To Kiki ~ C P

To my sister Alex Macnaughton ~ T M

Copyright © 2009 by Good Books, Intercourse, PA 17534
International Standard Book Number: 978-1-56148-659-5

Library of Congress Catalog Card Number: 2008033190

Text copyright © Caroline Pitcher 2009
Illustrations copyright © Tina Macnaughton 2009
Original edition published in English by Little Tiger Press,
an imprint of Magi Publications, London, England, 2009.

Printed in Singapore

Library of Congress Cataloging-in-Publication Data:

Pitcher, Caroline.

Time for bed, little one / Caroline Pitcher ; illustrated by Tina Macnaughton.

p. cm.

Summary: Little Fox gets permission to stay up past his dawn bedtime and play, but the other
animals he meets are either too tired to stay up, or busy with their daytime activities.

ISBN 978-1-56148-659-5 (hardcover : alk. paper)

[1. Bedtime--Fiction. 2. Foxes--Fiction. 3. Forest animals--Fiction.
4. Nocturnal animals--Fiction.] I. Macnaughton, Tina, ill. II. Title.

PZ7.P6427Tht 2009

[E]--dc22

2008033190

Time for Bed, Little One

Caroline Pitcher   Tina Macnaughton

Good Books

Intercourse, PA 17534
800/762-7171
www.GoodBooks.com

"Time for bed, little one," said Mother Fox.
"The moon is melting away and the sun is getting up.
It's time foxes were asleep."

"But I'm not sleepy!" Little Fox said. "My friends
are just waking. Please can I play a little while longer?"

"A few more minutes then, little cub."

So Little Fox scampered off into the woods where an owl was flying softly overhead.

"Hello, Owl! Will you play with me?" asked Fox.

"I'm on my way home to bed," hooted Owl. "And you should be too-hoo!"

"But I'm not sleepy!" Little Fox cried. And he charged into a woodland glade where Fawn was waking up.

"Play with me?" asked Little Fox.

"It's breakfast time for us," said gentle Mother Deer. "Shouldn't you be going home? The sun is turning the sky to gold, and foxes should be down in their dens."

"But I'm not sleepy!" Little Fox cried, and he skipped away again.

As Fox raced into the sunshine, a butterfly fluttered past his nose.

He bounded after it, jumping and bouncing, all the way to the riverbank.

Someone was busy in the water.

It was Otter! He was twisting and turning in
the rippling river, rolling through the bubbles.
"Will you play with me?" called Little Fox.
But Otter squeaked, "I'm busy now. I'm
catching fish, and dragonflies too."

"Otter's allowed to stay up all day,"
thought Little Fox. "*He* doesn't have
to go to sleep and miss everything."

Just then an acorn rolled
across the grass near Fox's paw.

He looked up and there was
Squirrel, high up on a branch.

"Catch me if you can!"
she cried and dashed
down the tree, shaking
her shimmering tail.

They raced into the
woods, through the
feathery ferns . . .

. . . scattering the
leaves and leaping
over logs.

The woods were rich with the smell of
flowers and fur and peppery leaves.
　But Little Fox was getting
tired and began to
trail behind.

"Please wait for me," he panted. "But I've got oodles of energy left," chattered Squirrel. "Maybe you should be going to bed."

Squirrel danced along the branch,
leaping from tree to tree all the
way through the woods.

Then it was quiet. Little Fox
was by himself.

"It's not fair," he thought. "When I get up tonight, there will be no one left awake. I'll be all alone again."

Little Fox sighed and padded home. He was so tired he could hardly even lift his head . . .

. . . and he nearly bumped into Badger!

"Are you off to bed, Little Fox?" Badger asked.

"I'm so tired, I can't wait to be snuggled in
my burrow. Will you be there when I get up? We
can play chase in the moonlight."

"Yes, oh yes, I will!" cried Fox,
and he trotted on home.
     At last he had a friend to
play with in the night.

Back in his den, Little Fox nestled down with
his mom. She nuzzled his ears and they cuddled
up safe—a cozy pile of paws and tails.

"Sleep well, my little one," his mother said.
"When the moon is high and the stars twinkle
in the dark, you'll wake up full of life again."
And Little Fox fell fast asleep.